CURSED

DESTINY FALLS

SHAW HART

 Created with Vellum

WANT A FREE BOOK?

You can grab Sweets Here.
Check out my website, www.shawhart.com for more free books!

This story starts with a curse.

Record Mason's whole life has been a curse, actually. At least that's what her parents have always told her.

It's kind of a long story.

She's sick of being a problem for her family and bringing them down with her bad luck though, so she packs up her old car and hits the road.

She's got a plan... kind of.

That plan comes to a screeching halt when her car breaks down just outside of Destiny Falls, Michigan.

Luckily for her, she has a friend that lives in town and after a call to the local mechanic, she's determined to get back on with her new life.

Then Gavin hops out of the tow truck.

She's into the sexy mechanic from the first moment, but she can't forget the curse. She's trying to get away from people so that she can't hurt them, so she needs to stay away from him at all costs.

Except Gavin doesn't seem to want her to.

When she tells him about the curse, he laughs in her face. Then he shows up the next day, determined to prove her wrong.

Will Gavin be able to break the curse, or is Record destined to a solitary existence?

ONE

Record

THIS STORY STARTS WITH A CURSE.

Actually, my life apparently started with a curse. Or as a curse. My parents like to mix it up and it gets confusing sometimes.

That's what I've been hearing my whole life anyway. My parents hadn't wanted kids. They were musicians and to hear them tell the story; they were days away from being discovered and making it big.

Then my dad broke up with his girlfriend, slept with my mom, and as the tale goes, his ex-girlfriend placed a curse on him.

I never really believed the story. Well, not all of it anyway. I was born eight months later, so either they got the dates wrong, or my dad was cheating on his girlfriend long before they broke up and she cursed him.

I had friends who used to tell me that it was all bullshit. That there wasn't a curse and that my parents were just blaming everything on me. I can't exactly argue with that, but when you grow up hearing about how you ruined everything, you kind of start to believe it.

So, when my car breaks down, sputtering and smoking as I steer it over to the side of the road, I'm not even surprised. Bad luck seems to follow me, so of course my car will crap out when I've only been on the road for a few hours.

I pull over right next to the Destiny Falls town sign and sigh. Looks like I'll be calling a tow truck. I know next to nothing about cars or engines and even if I did, it might not be safe to try to fix it myself. I'm liable to break something or injure myself in some way.

I grab my phone and pull up Google to search for the nearest mechanic shop when it hits me.

Destiny Falls.

That's the town that my college friend, Madelyn is from. I think she and Flynn moved back up here after graduation.

I bite my lip. I've barely talked to her since graduation. We've been texting, but that's about it. Would it be weird for me to call her? I mean, I would love to see her while I'm stuck here.

I pull up her number and hit dial before I can second guess myself. Madelyn was my suitemate in college. She had the room next to me in the dorms and she used to let me hang out over there when my roommate had company or got to be a little too much.

It was always her and Flynn and I wonder if they've realized that they're in love with each other yet. I smile at that thought. It was always painfully obvious that they were crazy about each other, but neither would admit it. They always insisted that they were just friends, but no one with eyes would believe that.

"Record!" Madelyn answers and I grin at her excitement.

"Madelyn!" I parrot back in the same tone and she laughs.

"It's been too long. I was just telling Flynn that we should call you or maybe make a trip down to Grand Rapids to see you."

"I'm actually not there anymore."

"Really? Did you get a new job? Did some rich patron offer to sponsor you so you can just paint all day?"

"No, not quite. I just needed a change of scenery."

"So, you finally got away from your parents then," she says flatly and I bite my bottom lip.

Madelyn and Flynn are the only ones that I've really opened up to about my family and even then, I only gave them the bare minimum of details. They don't know any of the truly terrible things that my curse has caused my family. It was still more than enough for both of them to hate my family and urge me to get away.

I want to tell her about everything that's been happening in the last two years. I used to think that when I went away to college, that the curse would follow me too and leave my family alone but that's not what happened.

My parents and sister have hated me for all of the bad luck that I've brought my family, and I can't say that I blame them.

My sister, Callie, has always been the golden child. She was the one that they planned, that they wanted. It's hard to be around them and see them be good parents to her.

Meanwhile, I'm treated as the family scapegoat.

All because of a curse that took place before I was even born.

Everything is always my fault in some way, and I just couldn't take it any longer. I knew that I had to leave, so I packed up everything in my tiny room and left. My parents and Callie would be better off without me and my bad luck in their lives.

My whole existence fits into two suitcases. I can't decide if that's sad or not.

I want to tell Madelyn that I left because I didn't want to be a burden or a pain on my family anymore, but it seems like maybe a face-to-face conversation, so instead I just say, "Yeah."

"Good for you, Rec. Where are you at now then?"

"My car just broke down next to the Destiny Falls town sign."

There's a moment of silence and then Madelyn is calling for Flynn. I pull the phone away from my ear as she screams excitedly about me being in town to him.

"We'll be right there! I'll call Gavin on the way. He's the mechanic and his shop is right by there, so he'll be there to get your car in a bit too."

"Thanks."

"Of course! I can't wait to see you again! Are you staying for long? Why didn't you tell me that you were coming?" She rattles off questions rapid-fire as I try to keep up.

"Ready to go?" I hear Flynn ask.

"Yeah. We'll be right there and then we can catch up," she says and I smile.

"Sounds good. See you soon."

We hang up, and I grab my purse and climb out of my old Mustang. I worked my butt off to buy her when I was twenty. She's my most prized possession and I hate to say it but I'm a little nervous to let her out of my sight.

My parents and sister were always trying to borrow her but I never trusted them to not damage my baby in some way. None of them were the best drivers.

A tow truck rumbles around the corner and I lift my hand, shielding my eyes from the sunlight as I try to make out if they're here for me or just passing by.

The truck slows and rolls to a stop in front of my Mustang, and I smile as a guy climbs out.

My smile drops quickly when I get a good look at the guy.

"Holy shit," I breathe as my eyes drink him in.

He's tall, dark, and handsome. His grease-stained shirt is clinging to his muscles and my mouth waters as I look him over. He has dark brown hair that's just a tad too long. It's hanging over his dark eyebrows and half shielding his eyes but there's no hiding those eyes.

They're blue, crystal blue and so focused on me that I start to squirm. I reach up, tucking my faded blue hair behind my ears self-consciously.

"Are you with Madelyn and Flynn?" he calls to me and oh my gosh that voice!

"Uh-huh," I mumble as his boots crunch on the dirt and rocks.

His jeans are hanging low on his hips and are just as streaked with grease as his shirt.

"I'm Gavin. They said that you need a tow?"

"Yeah, it just started making this clunking sound and then the engine went," I tell him.

I clear my throat and try to get my mind out of the gutter.

"Let's take a look."

I watch as he opens my car door and bends down to pop the hood. My eyes zero in on his ass and my face flames.

Abort! This is never going to happen. You're not even staying that long and you're not dating. You're going to figure out your life first. Do not get attached to him!

"Could be your fan belt, but I'm guessing it's more likely the distributor cap. Actually, I think it's both," he says as he pokes around under the hood.

"Is that a hard fix?" I ask.

I'm already trying to figure how much of my savings I'll have to dip into to fix this.

"No, it's not hard to fix, but it might be hard to find the parts for a classic car like this," he admits.

He looks up and his blue eyes pin me to the ground.

"Oh," I say lamely and he studies me for a moment before he goes back to looking at my car.

"I'll tow it to my shop and look for parts. I should be able to get something in soon. Maybe a couple of days."

"Okay. Thanks," I say.

It's not like I have much of a choice. I need my car if I want to make it to Sault Ste. Marie. I've rented a cabin there and I'm going to paint and try to sell my art at the farmers' market and craft sales that they do there.

I figure that I can make that work for two months or so before I have to figure out a new way to make money.

I sigh and Gavin looks over at me with a frown.

"It shouldn't take me that long to fix," he assures me, and I nod.

"Thanks."

Flynn and Madelyn pull up then and I grin as I see Madelyn bouncing in the passenger seat.

"Are they together yet?" I ask Gavin, and he gives me a grin.

"Yeah. They finally admitted how they felt like a month ago."

"It's about time," I say, and he nods in agreement.

I can feel him eyeing me but I'm too focused on my friends as they climb out of their car. Madelyn runs at me, wrapping me up in a hug as I laugh.

"I can't believe that you're here!" she says and I step back, only for Flynn to pull me into a hug next.

"It's good to see you again," he says with a grin.

"You too. I've missed you guys."

"Are you all set with your car?" Madelyn asks and I nod, turning back to Gavin.

"Yeah, Gavin said that he can fix it," I say and he stares right at me.

I wish that I could tell what he was thinking.

"I can fix it," he says with a dip of his chin.

I don't know why, but the way he says it sounds like he's going to fix more than just my car.

"Great! We'll give you a ride. We can show you around town," Madelyn says as she takes my hand and leads me over to their car.

I take one last look at Gavin before I climb into the back seat. Flynn and Madelyn wave as we drive back toward downtown Destiny Falls and I try to pay attention to the sights, but all I can think and wonder about is the sexy mechanic.

TWO

Record

"I WISH that you had told us that you were coming up this way," Madelyn says as she lets us into her house. "Flynn and I rented a cabin up in Honey Peak for this weekend, so we won't be around much."

"Sorry, it was kind of a last-minute decision," I tell her as I look around the place.

She lives in a nice two-story house just a block over from the water. The whole house is bright and welcoming, just like Flynn and Madelyn. It makes me feel at home as soon as I step inside.

"Well, you're more than welcome to stay here while we're gone. All of the cabins over by the Mystery Cabin have been rented and the hotel in town isn't really that great," she says with a scrunch of her nose.

"Thanks, that would be perfect."

She shows me around the house and where my guest

room is, and it's only then that I realize that I never grabbed my suitcases out of the back of my car.

"Crap," I mumble and I look over to see Madelyn smiling at me.

I'm guessing that she just figured out that I forgot it too.

"You can borrow my car while you're here. Gavin's mechanic shop is only a few blocks from here. I'll text you the address," she says, and I give her a grateful smile.

"You're a lifesaver," I tell her, wrapping my arms around her.

She just laughs and shrugs me off.

"Are you hungry? I have girls' night tonight, but I can always eat twice," she says. "I think that I have time for something quick."

Madelyn already told me about girls' night and invited me along but I'm too tired to stay up late tonight. Not after I've been driving for most of the day. She had offered to stay home with me, but I know that I won't be much company. She's already letting me crash at her place for a few days and use her car. I'm determined not to take away her time with her friends as well.

"No, I'm tired after driving all day. I'll just grab my luggage and a sandwich or something on the way back here."

"Sounds good. You can text me if you need anything."

I nod and she gives me a quick hug before she heads back downstairs. My phone dings a second later and I tense.

My parents and sister have been texting and calling me all day. I haven't been answering but that doesn't seem to be deterring them.

I know what they want. They want me to come back. They want me to be their maid and ATM and I can't do it anymore. I can't pay for the mistakes that I didn't intentionally cause. I know that they'll say that I owe it to them because it's my curse, my existence, that caused it, and I can't hear that anymore.

I figured that everyone would be better off if I wasn't around. That's why I'm going to try to stick to myself while I'm in town. It will be nice to see Madelyn and Flynn again, but I'm better by myself.

I need to be on my own so that I can't hurt anyone else.

That was the thought that I kept having every day for the last six months. Then one day it hit me.

If I wanted my family to be safe and better off, then I needed to leave them. Sure, I might be lonely and they might struggle without my money but I could try to send some back, once I get my new place and save up a bit. Besides, without all of my bad luck there, I'm sure that my mom and dad will be able to find full-time work soon.

I know that I'm hoping that without me there, they'll miss me and that either their luck will stay bad and it won't matter that I'm cursed or that they'll say they miss me too much and don't care about me ruining everything. I have a feeling that it's a long shot, but I still can't stop hoping that it happens.

I take a deep breath and steel myself before I pull my phone out. That breath comes out in a relieved rush when I see that it's a message from Madelyn instead.

She sent me the address for the mechanic shop and I glance out the window. The sun is just starting to set and I really am tired. If I go right now, I could grab my bags, come back here for a shower, and then pass out for the night.

My fingers clench tight around my phone when it starts to ring and I see my sister's name on the screen. I hit ignore and grab the keys that Madelyn left for me off of the dresser before I jog downstairs.

It doesn't take me long to reach Gavin's Mechanic Shop, and I smile as I park right out front. I grew up in Grand Rapids and went to college in Lansing, so I'm used to traffic and loud sounds.

I kind of like it here in this sleepy little town though. There's no traffic, three people waved at me on the way here and I feel relaxed after staring at the water for half of my drive here.

"Hey, I was just about to text Flynn and let him know that your luggage was here," Gavin says as I climb out of the car.

"Yeah, Madelyn showed me my room and I figured it out then."

He just nods and turns to head back inside, and I smile slightly as I follow after him.

He's wearing a stained pair of overalls now, *Gavin's Mechanic Shop* and the logo plastered on his back and his name stitched over the left pocket. Most people look terrible in them, but Gavin wears them well.

I need to stop. I can't stay here. It's not nearly enough distance between my family. Plus, there's the curse to think about. I can't get close to him or anyone. I wouldn't be able to live with myself if he got hurt because of me.

Besides, it's not like the stoic, grumpy guy in front of me is showing any interest in me anyway.

I push some of my blue hair out of my face as I follow him into the open bay area. A fan by the door immediately blows all of my hair right back into my face and I sigh.

I step out of the way of the fan and try to right my hair as Gavin watches me.

"Did you have any luck finding the part?" I ask him as I fidget with the hem of my shirt.

There's just something about having his blue eyes on

me that makes me squirm. It feels like I'm burning up and I don't know why.

"Not yet. I looked around town and the next few towns over but they didn't have it. I have a few more feelers out and I've started looking online. I think I found a place that has it but it will be more expensive from there, so I was trying to find a cheaper option."

"Thanks," I say.

I definitely don't have the money to spend on fixing my car if it's going to cost thousands. I'm almost afraid to ask how much he thinks it will be, so instead, I look around the shop for my luggage.

"I put your things in my office," he tells me and then he's walking by me and inside the small waiting area of the shop.

"Okay," I say, dragging out the word as I turn to follow him.

We head down a short hallway and pass by a bathroom on one side. His office is at the end of the hallway and I follow him inside.

That was a mistake because the space is tiny. Gavin turns around with my suitcase and duffel bag and we collide. I try to sidestep him but there's nowhere to go, so I end up backing up out into the hallway.

I look like an idiot and my face flames as I look away from him and down to my luggage.

"Thanks," I mumble and he just grunts.

"I'll see you later," I say as I spin on my heel and practically sprint out the front door.

My suitcase bangs on the door behind me, and I don't dare look back. I unlock Madelyn's car and toss my things into the back seat before I hurry to climb behind the wheel.

It isn't until I've started the car that I get the strength to look back to the shop. Gavin is back in the open bay area, his arms crossed over his chest as he stares at me.

He's looking at me like I'm some sort of puzzle that he can't figure out. I stare back at him.

I want him to figure me out. No one has ever taken much of an interest in me. No one has really cared what I was thinking, but I get the feeling that he does.

Maybe I should tell him. I could warn him to not get too close to me, that all I ever do is ruin people's lives, but when I open my mouth, my throat feels dry and I know that I would never be able to get the words out.

So instead, I push the car into reverse and take one last look at Gavin before I turn and head back down Main Street.

THREE

Record

THERE'S a note from Madelyn on the counter when I wake up the next morning. I yawn as I pick it up, rubbing sleep from my eyes as I try to make out her loopy hand-writing.

RECORD,

HOPE THAT YOU SLEPT ALRIGHT! *I'm headed into the market to make sure that everything is taken care of and then Flynn and I are going to head up to our cabin rental. Flynn talked to Gavin last night and he said that it would be a few days so we'll see you when we get back on Sunday!*

.   .   .

FEEL *free to take my car anywhere and eat anything that you want in the fridge or pantry! I told my friends that you were in town and they all want to meet you, so if you need anything, you can give them a call!*

SEE YOU SUNDAY!
   Madelyn

IRIS – *555- 0157*
   Sutton – 555- 0195
   Lyla – 555- 0186
   Gavin – 555- 0117

I SMILE at her thoughtfulness and grab a magnet so that I can hang the note up on the fridge.

It's been a while since I had a girls' night or a lot of friends and part of me wants to meet them, but I know that I won't be staying in town for long. Maybe it's better if I don't. That way I don't have to worry about my curse rubbing off on them.

I open the fridge and smile when I see that it's fully stocked. I have a feeling that Flynn did this last night while I was sleeping. I passed out after I got back with my stuff. I could barely keep my eyes open in the shower and when I couldn't find my pajamas, I just put on an old paint-splattered shirt and some underwear and called it good. Luckily for me, I was more awake when I got dressed this morning.

Now I'm feeling more well-rested. It looks like I'll be in town for a few days, so maybe I get dressed and see some of the sights. Or I could sit out on the porch here and read a book. It might be safer for everyone if I stayed by myself. It's been a while since I last laid around for a whole day. I was always working at least one job and painting in my free time. Not that I regret that. It allowed me to save up so that I could get out on my own.

I snag a muffin from the container on the counter and take a bite as I head over to the front windows.

"Hey!" a pretty purple-haired girl says, popping up right in front of me and giving me a heart attack. "You must be Record!"

I stare at her wide eyed and that's when I see the pink and red-haired girls standing behind her.

"We're Madelyn's friends," the pink-haired girl says, and I lift a hand to wave at them weakly.

"Uh, hi."

They wave back and head for the front door and I try to calm my racing heart as I move to let them in.

"Hey! I'm Lyla," the purple-haired one says. "And this is Sutton and Iris," she says, nodding to the pink and red-haired girls in turn.

"Hey, it's nice to meet you."

"I love your hair," Lyla says as they come into the house and I smile.

"Thanks. I like yours too."

"I need to dye it again. It's starting to fade already. Maybe I'll try blue this time."

"Yeah, I need to touch up mine too. I love the color, but it fades so fast," I tell her as we all head into the kitchen.

"Madelyn and Flynn left," I inform them.

"We know. We wanted to come meet you before we had to head to work," Sutton says.

"Yeah, Madelyn told me that you own the antiques store in town," I say to Iris and she nods.

Lyla passes her a muffin and grabs another for herself.

"We work at the Mystery Cabin. I don't know if you want to do any touristy thing while you're here, but we could take you over there if you want," Sutton says with a smile as Lyla hands her a muffin too.

"Yeah, I was just thinking that I should try to poke around town today. I didn't have any concrete plans though."

"Let us take you over there. You can check out the cabin and then we can take you out for lunch," Lyla says.

I bite my lip. These girls are really nice and I already like them. I don't want to put them in harm's way though with my curse.

"Let's go!" Lyla says, making the decision for me and I grab my phone and Madelyn's keys off the counter before she drags me out the front door.

"I've got to meet Arlo and get into the shop, but I'll see you guys at lunch," Iris says with a wave.

"See you!" Sutton and Lyla call back as they take me over to a Jeep parked behind Madelyn's car in the driveway.

"Madelyn says that you like to paint," Sutton says as Lyla starts the car and reverses out of the drive.

"Yeah, I love it. I was actually coming up here to see if I could sell my art at the farmers' markets or they have this big craft sale in Sault Ste. Marie for like the month of July," I say as we head down Main Street.

Maybe I should add that I also picked it because it's a

solitary habit and I don't have to worry about hurting or cursing anyone while I do it, but I leave that part out.

"That's so cool! We'll have to go check it out," Lyla says as she stops at a red light.

"They're opening a new ceramics place in Lilac Harbor soon too. We could check that out too. Have you ever gone to a place like that?" Sutton asks, twisting in her seat to face me more.

"I've only done ceramics a few times, but it was cool."

"So as long as it's paint, you love it then?" Lyla asks with an infectious grin and I laugh.

"Pretty much."

"Oh, there's Hudson!" Lyla says, waving at a dark-haired man outside of some restaurant. "That's my boyfriend."

He waves back, blowing her a kiss, and I smile. I've always dreamed about finding my soulmate but it hasn't happened. With the curse, I'm not sure that I would risk getting close to anyone.

"When did Madelyn and Flynn finally get together?" I ask and Sutton and Lyla both groan and roll their eyes.

"Like a month ago."

"It took ages," Lyla groans and I grin at her dramatics.

"Yeah, I kept waiting for one of them to say it in college, but they never did."

"Oh yeah! I keep forgetting that you knew them when they first met. Was it love at first sight?" Sutton asks.

"Absolutely. They were both hooked but too chicken to say anything to the other. I thought for sure when we graduated that they would be forced to say it, but instead, Flynn just said that he was going to start his own company and Madelyn offered to have him move back here with her."

"And then eighteen months later, they finally get

together," Sutton says as we head out of the downtown area and farther along the coast.

"How did they finally admit it?" I ask.

"Flynn got a job in Los Angeles and was going to take it. She admitted that she loved him before he could," Sutton says.

"I'm surprised that he was going to leave her."

"Well, actually they slept together, and she freaked out and said it was a mistake and then he was going to leave, so she told him."

"Ah, yeah, that makes more sense."

Sutton and Lyla laugh as we slow and turn into a gravel parking lot. The place looks like an old cabin. It's an A-frame with a bright red door and a sign on the side that proclaims that we've reached the world-famous Mystery Cabin.

"You work here?" I ask as we park and climb out.

"Yeah. My great uncle owns it. We're in the gift shop," Sutton says, leading me to the back door.

They enter first and I look around as I follow them. There's a mini putt-putt golf course off to the side and a sign leading to a zip line farther back. I don't know what I was expecting from a place called the Mystery Cabin, but it wasn't this.

We head inside and I look around the gift shop. The place screams tourist trap, but I still love it.

"Welcome to the Mystery Cabin!" an old man in a suit says, waving his arms out wide to encompass the glory that is the gift shop.

"She's with us, Stan," Lyla says and the man's smile dims and falls in an instant.

"Good. I'm grabbing something to eat," he says, turning

but Lyla stops him and hands him a muffin that she must have taken from Madelyn's house.

"Was thinking of you," she says, batting her eyes at him and he just grunts out a thanks before he heads out of a side door.

The gift shop door opens and a black and white dog sprints in.

"Bandit!" Sutton calls and the dog skids to a stop and turns to head behind the counter.

"Sorry, he's got so much energy in the morning," Sutton says but I just smile.

"It's no problem. I love dogs. I just wasn't expecting one to come bursting through the door," I say with a laugh.

"Sorry, that was my fault. I didn't know that we had guests already," a tall guy in a backward baseball hat says as he comes inside.

"Record, this is my boyfriend and the Mystery Cabin's handyman, Teller. Teller, this is Record. She's Madelyn and Flynn's friend from college and she's here for a visit," Sutton says.

"Nice to meet you," he says, shaking my hand before he heads behind the counter to drop a kiss on Sutton's lips.

"Ready for that tour?" Lyla asks, wiggling her eyebrows at me and I grin.

"Let's do it."

FOUR

Record

LYLA AND SUTTON invited me out to dinner with them, but I told them another time. We've been hanging out all day and while nothing bad has happened, that doesn't mean that it's not coming.

I figured that it wasn't worth tempting fate.

I'm pretty sure that they wanted to spend some time alone with their boyfriends anyway, so that's how I end up driving down the half-deserted streets toward Gavin's Mechanic Shop.

I told myself that I'm only going to go and check on my car's progress, but I can't deny that there are butterflies in my stomach at the thought of seeing Gavin again.

I don't know what's gotten into me, but it's like ever since I met him, I can't help but try to find new ways or excuses to be around him.

It's getting late, the sun is just starting to set, and I wonder if he'll even still be at the shop. Maybe he had a date tonight or was planning on hanging out with friends or something. Hell, he could even be out picking up someone else's car that stalled out.

My stomach drops at the thought of him out on a date and I try to ignore the feeling as I turn off of Main Street and head toward his shop. His place isn't far but now that it's starting to get dark, I'm wondering if I should have driven instead of walked. It was just so nice out and I didn't think that it would take me long but I got distracted by some of the shops downtown and now I'm wondering if they have an Uber or anything here. I probably shouldn't be walking around at night.

It doesn't take long to get there and a smile tips my lips when I spot his tow truck out front. One of the bays is still open and there are lights on inside so I head in that direction.

"Hey," I call as I reach the door and he glances over at me.

It's the same as every other time those bright blue eyes land on me and I suck in a breath as my heart takes off like a shot.

He's wearing his usual dark blue overalls but they're unzipped and hanging at his waist. He's got a white shirt on that's covered in grease stains and I don't know where to look first.

My fingers itch for a paintbrush and canvas, but I doubt that I could ever truly capture this scene onto canvas. It would always be missing something.

"Careful," he says, nodding toward some car parts at my feet.

"Thanks," I say as I tiptoe around them.

"I found the belt for your car a few towns over and I ordered that today so it should be in tomorrow or the day after, but I'm still looking for distributor cap," he tells me as he bends over the hood of some old pickup truck.

"Any luck finding one online?"

He shrugs, his big shoulder lifting and falling distractedly as he finishes tightening something under the hood. I move closer, looking down into the depths of the engine but it's all just the same metal pieces or rubber tubes.

"I don't know how you know what each of these things does. Cars always seemed so confusing to me."

"Nah," he says, finally standing back up. "They're all pretty much the same. Same pieces, same concept that makes them work. That's why I like them. They're easy to figure out once you know what you're doing."

He sets his wrench down and picks up a tiny metal piece before he ducks back under the hood.

"When did you get into cars?" I ask when he comes back up.

"In high school. I loved shop class, but my dad was always into cars and I probably learned more from him over the years than that class."

"Was he a mechanic too?"

"No, he was a psychiatrist."

He grabs his wrench again and I watch as he screws a bolt back into place.

"Are you from Destiny Falls?"

"No, I moved up here right after I graduated. We used to come by here on family vacations and I always loved the area. When I found out that the old owner of this mechanic shop was retiring, I jumped at the chance to buy it from him."

"So you've been here for like eight years then?"

I would guess that he's not quite thirty yet.

He nods. "Yeah, around there, I guess."

I get the feeling that if it's not cars, he doesn't really want to talk about it. Unfortunately, I know next to nothing about cars.

"What about you?" he asks and I blink at him.

"What about me?"

"Where are you from?"

"Originally, Howell, Michigan, but we moved to Grand Rapids when I was like four and that's where I grew up."

"Did you like it?"

I pause.

Did I like it?

The town was fine, there was always something to do, but I wasn't happy. I think that had more to do with my family than the city though. I mean, can anyone who's cursed really be happy?

He's still watching me and I swallow.

"It was fine. I didn't love the traffic, but there was lots to do and see."

He nods, but I get the feeling that he can see more than I said.

"Did you get that from your dad? That dissecting look?" I blurt out and to my surprise, he cracks a smile.

His whole face lights up and I rock back on my heels as his bright eyes land on me.

"I suppose. Not a lot got past him. He was good at seeing more than surface-level things."

"Sounds like a good psychiatrist then. Or a good police detective," I try to joke and he grins.

"Yeah, he was. He retired a few years ago and now he and my mom travel a lot."

"That must be nice."

He shrugs and grabs a rag at his feet to wipe his hands off.

"Where did you grow up then?" I ask him as he reaches up to close the hood of the truck.

"Chicago."

"Really?" I ask and he grins at my shocked tone.

"Yep."

"I can't picture you in a big city."

"Yeah, I prefer the small town. Less crime and traffic."

I nod and he starts to gather up his tools.

"Are you closing up now? I wasn't sure what your hours were."

"Yeah, I think that I'm done for the day. Have you eaten?"

"Uh, no. I mean, Lyla and Sutton invited me to dinner, but I know that they wanted to see their boyfriends, and so I took a raincheck."

I wince. Why did I just tell him all of that? It in no way answered his question.

"Is that what you did today? Hang out with the girls?"

"Yeah, they took me to the Mystery Cabin for a tour," I say and he smiles. "And then we had lunch and I got to see Iris's shop this afternoon."

"How did you like town?"

"I love it. Everyone is so nice and there's no traffic or long waits at the restaurants. Plus, the water! Though I didn't really get to go down to the beach that much today."

He smiles softly as I go on about the town and I close my mouth.

"We can go now. It will be dark, but the lights from the bridge and boats should help."

I bite my bottom lip. I want to take him up on his offer so bad, but I can't. Not unless I want the curse to get him too.

"Record," he says softly, and I blink at him as he takes a step toward me and then another.

His hand cups my face, and I lean into his touch. How long has it been since someone has touched me? After Madelyn hugging me, I can't even remember.

His mouth lowers to mine and I lick my lips. I know that I shouldn't let him kiss me. We barely know each other and I'm cursed, but I want this.

I want him.

His lips lands on mine and I close my eyes.

FIVE

Record

HIS MOUTH COMES DOWN on to mine and I suck in a breath. I've only been kissed twice before and neither time went well. The first time Bobby Meyers's braces cut my lip, leaving me bleeding all over the both of us. The second time, Ray Calder had kissed me so hard that our teeth knocked together and I ended up chipping one of his. After that I just let the curse win and tried to stay away from boys, but I can't do that here. Not with Gavin.

His kiss isn't like either of the other two. He's gentle, his hands coming up to cradle my face, and he angles my head, kissing me deeper.

My lips part for him when his tongue slips along the seam of my mouth and he deepens the kiss even more as my tongue starts to tangle with his.

"Gavin," I breathe, gripping his shirt as the world starts to move under my feet.

At least that's how it feels anyway.

His hands tighten on my chin, the other slipping around the back of my neck, and I give him complete control of me. He tastes like coffee and apples, and I moan as his tongue tangles with mine.

He moves closer, his body pressing firmly against me as he conquers my mouth. His teeth nip at my bottom lip and my breath hitches at the sensation. My body is screaming for me to do more, to feel more of him against me.

He nips at my bottom lip again, his tongue coming out to soothe the sting, and I whimper with need.

I'm so close.

I don't even know what that thought means, but as Gavin presses against me, a coil tightens even further in my body, low in my belly.

"Record," he breathes out and I sigh.

I want to hear him say my name like over and over again.

"Record," he moans again and I blink my eyes open.

Record, all you do is hurt people.

That thought hits me and I jerk away from Gavin and he blinks at me. His fingers are still holding a lock of my hair and I reach up to pull it away from him so that I can get out of here but he tightens his grip.

"Record," he says.

I shake my head. "Don't."

"Yes," he says back firmly and I suck in a shaky breath.

I know that that voice, those words, are my family. I've heard my mother and father tell me that a million times over the years.

I hurt people and I really like Gavin. I can't hurt him too.

"I like you," I start and he takes a step closer.

"I like you too. That's why I kissed you."

He's so blunt and it has my lips curling but I stop when I remember what I'm about to tell him.

"Do you believe in curses?"

"What?"

"Do you believe in curses?"

"No, there's no such thing."

"Yes, there is. I'm cursed," I whisper and he stares at me for a beat before he throws his head back and laughs.

"I am!" I insist and he only laughs harder.

I glare at him, taking a step back when I realize that he's no longer holding on to my hair, and then I turn and bolt for the door.

The laughter cuts off immediately and a second later, I'm being lifted off the ground.

"Nope. You're not walking home. It's dark out and I know that you walked here," he growls in my ear as I squirm to get out of his hold.

"I'm not getting in the car with you," I snap, and he chuckles.

"Because of the curse?"

"It's real!"

"No, it's not, but don't worry. We're going to talk all about that."

He carries me over to a workbench and grabs a set of keys out of the drawer there before he carries me outside and over to a new-looking Jeep.

"I can walk," I tell him stormily.

"But the curse," he says back sarcastically.

I try to kick him but he dodges me, and I seethe.

He's not taking this seriously, but he will when something bad happens.

He opens the passenger door and sets me inside.

"I like you a little less now," I inform him, and he just grins at me.

"No, you don't."

He closes the door and I glare at him as he heads around the hood and climbs behind the wheel.

"So tell me about this curse," he says as we pull out of the parking lot.

"You mean the curse that you don't believe in?"

"That's the one."

I debate telling him, but maybe if I can explain it to him, he'll get it and he'll stay away from me for his own safety.

A piece of my heart breaks at the thought of him avoiding me, but it's for the best.

"I've been cursed since I was born."

He glances over at me and I take a deep breath before I go on.

"My parents were musicians, and they had finally caught a break when they found out that they were pregnant with me. They had to turn down the record deal to raise me."

"So they named you Record?"

"Yeah, they said that I was supposed to be their replacement. Something just as good as a label wanting to sign them, but I wasn't. I've done nothing but mess things up for my parents and sister ever since."

"How?" he asks, his fingers tightening around the steering wheel.

Good. He's finally taking this seriously.

"Lots of stuff. They had to work to raise us and they hated their jobs. When I fell and broke my arm, my dad came to the hospital and missed a meeting with a big client and ended up losing his job."

"That's not your fault," he starts, but I go on.

"I've broken a lot of bones. I have a ton of bad luck and that's spread over the years to my family."

"How?" he asks, his voice hard with frustration.

"My mom and dad have both gotten fired from numerous jobs," I start.

"So they're bad workers then," he counters.

"One of our houses burned down," I tell him.

"Probably from a candle that they lit or something electrical, so either way, not your fault."

"We never won anything," I list off. "Not on lottery tickets or at the casino or even things at school."

"So? Lots of people never win stuff. I would argue most don't and most certainly never win the lottery."

"We lost houses and apartments. Been in car accidents."

I'm listing off more and more things, desperate for him to see my point, and I don't even know why. He wasn't there for all of those things. He doesn't know how much it hurt all of us.

"None of that was because of you or a curse," he says, and I shake my head.

He pulls into Madelyn's driveway and I hurry to unbuckle and get out.

"Hey," he says, his hand resting on my arm. "You didn't cause any of that. They did. They didn't work hard, they slacked off, or they lied and got caught. Your family, they're just blaming you for everything. None of those things were your fault or a curse's fault."

I open my mouth to argue with him, but his jaw is set and I know that he's never going to believe me.

"It's just bad luck or the consequences of their own actions, Record," he says softly and I feel tears sting the back of my eyes.

"I have to go," I choke out. "But you should stay away from me. For your own good."

I climb out of the Jeep and run up the front porch steps and inside.

I lean back against the door, tears slipping free from my eyes, and wait for him to leave. It takes a few minutes, but finally his headlights reverse and head back down the street.

SIX

Record

I DIDN'T THINK that Gavin would really stay away from me. Maybe I just didn't want him to, but either way, what I wasn't expecting was for him to be knocking on the front door bright and early the next day.

"What are you doing here?" I ask him, and he grins at me.

"I'm going to prove to you that you're not cursed."

I blink at him, wondering if I'm still dreaming or something but nope. Gavin is standing on Madelyn's front porch in a pair of swim trunks and a dark blue T-shirt.

"No," I say, trying to close the door, but he catches it before I can.

"What do you have to lose? Let me take you out. Either you prove that you're right or I do."

"And when I'm right? Will you stay away from me?"

"Yeah, sure," he says, but I can tell that he's not happy about it.

"Fine."

"Good. Now get dressed. You're going to need a swim-suit and comfortable shoes."

I open the door and let him inside before I head up the stairs. I need to get away from him so that I can think this through and calm my racing heart.

I should tell him that I can't go, maybe make up some excuse or some fake plans. I'm betting that he would just call Lyla, Sutton, or Iris though to confirm my plans and find out that I was lying.

Looks like this is happening.

I'll just try to make sure that nothing bad happens to him. I'll keep my distance and everything will be fine.

I have to dig through my suitcases to find my swimsuit. I tug that on, pulling on a loose-fitting summer dress over it. I have a pair of slip-on flip-flops and I shove my feet into them before I head back downstairs.

"I just want to warn you again—" I start as I come down the stairs and he grabs my hand, cutting me off as he pulls me outside.

"Yeah, yeah, that you're cursed and something bad is going to happen. I'll take my chances."

"You should take this seriously!" I argue as he pulls me over to his Jeep.

"Oh, I am," he says. My heart kicks against my ribcage as his blue eyes meet mine.

He helps me into the passenger seat and then climbs behind the wheel.

"Where are you taking me?" I ask him as he heads toward town.

"I've today all planned out. We're going to go zip-lining, parasailing, kayaking, jet-skiing, and we're grabbing a bite to eat."

"Are you crazy! We're going to get hurt. Or one of us is going to die!" I argue as I turn to grab the door handle.

"No, we're not. Well, we're not as long as you don't jump out of a moving car!" he says, grabbing my hand and tugging me back into the seat before I can get to the door.

"Are you crazy?" I ask him again and he shakes his head.

"No, and you're not cursed."

"Okay, but I tell you that I'm cursed and you decide to test it out by doing a ton of dangerous things. That seems pretty crazy to me."

"It's the fastest way to make you see that you're not cursed."

I fold my arms over my chest as we start to head down the coast. When he pulls up outside of the Mystery Cabin, I'm a little surprised.

Maybe this won't be that scary.

Teller greets us as we pull up, and I wave at him as I hop out.

"Hey, you two," he greets us and I stand closer to him.

Gavin rolls his eyes at me, and Teller just grins.

"Ready to go?"

"Go where?" I ask.

"Zip-lining," Teller says as he starts to walk toward the woods.

I glare at Gavin, and he grabs my hand and pulls me along after him.

The zip-lining course at the Mystery Cabin isn't very big or very tall and I let out a deep breath as Teller hooks Gavin and me into harnesses and goes over the rules.

"So, you just walk off the platform. You want to get a good push so that you don't get stuck halfway across. Then once you're close to the other side, you tug on this strap to slow down. I'll be over there to catch you," Teller assures me, and I nod.

"We got this," Gavin says, and the guys fist bump before Teller heads off down the line to the next platform.

"I hate you," I tell him, and he smirks at me.

"So, you want me to go first then?"

"Not a chance."

He laughs as I get a running start and push off of the platform. I suck in a breath as I go weightless but the harness catches me and soon I'm flying through the air. I laugh as I get halfway, and I can see Gavin cheering from behind me.

I look forward and realize that I'm close to Teller, so I tug on the strap. Teller catches me as I come to a stop and he high-fives me.

"How was that?" he asks.

"So cool," I tell him, a wide grin stretching my lips.

I never thought that I would do anything like that. How could I when I was cursed? I'm glad that I did though.

I turn to watch Gavin go next, and soon we're both laughing on the other platform.

"Ready to do the next one?" Teller asks as he moves the lines to the next run.

"Sure," I say, and Teller hooks his own harness up and takes off.

"Not so scary, huh?" Gavin asks, and I shrug.

"No, I guess not."

"Still think that you're cursed."

"Yep. That was just one time. It could happen next time."

"Something bad could happen to anyone next time," he tells me, and I look away from him.

I think that he's right...

I don't tell him that. Instead, I wait for Teller to signal me and then I take off, flying through the air again.

We finish up the zip lining course pretty fast. It's only four different runs and we're done in under an hour.

"Thanks," I tell Teller and he just nods.

"Have fun!" he calls as Gavin takes my hand and leads me back to the Jeep.

"Where to next?" I ask him, and he grins as we head back toward town.

"Parasailing."

I shake my head at him as he heads past Destiny Falls and over toward Maple Bend. I watch the beach go by until I see the signs for parasailing.

"This is a bad idea," I groan as he drags me from the car.

"This is the best idea. Come on."

I let him lead me over to the little stand and watch as he pays, and then we're heading over to a small speedboat.

"Hey! I'm Jax," the guy says as he grabs two harnesses from a box by the boat. "I'll be the captain today."

We listen to his instructions as he gets us hooked into our harnesses and then we're holding on to the metal bar as the boat pulls away from the dock.

My heart is beating hard now. I'm more afraid than when we went zip-lining and I wonder if it's because we're going to be a lot higher in the air or if because I had Teller and Sutton and Lyla nearby for the last thing.

Now it's just Gavin and I and this boat.

"Scared?" Gavin yells over the wind.

"Terrified," I admit, nodding.

"You'll be fine!" Jax yells and I want to flip him off, but he tells us to get into position.

We move back slightly to the little stand and my palms feel sweaty on the bar.

"We should not be doing this," I say, but it's too late to protest.

The kite takes off, and soon we're way up in the air.

"Oh my gosh, oh my gosh, oh my gosh," I shout and Gavin laughs next to me.

"You're doing great!" he yells and I'm too afraid to look away from the water way down below us to glare at him.

"I hate you!" I yell back instead, and he reaches over, squeezing my fingers before he grabs hold of the bar once more.

After a while, I start to relax but I never quite unwind like I did with the zip lining. We land back on the little stand and Jax flashes us a smile and a thumbs-up before he turns the boat back to the dock.

Gavin drags me up onto the dock when we get back, and I lean on him. My legs feel like jelly and Jax just smirks.

"Did you have fun?" he asks us and I stare at him until he laughs.

"The next time will be even better," he promises me, and I look over to Gavin as we turn to leave.

"Never again," I tell him and he just tugs me closer against him.

I thought that we would get back in the car, but he just leads me farther down the dock to a jet ski rental shack.

"This should be more your speed," he says as he passes me a life vest and tugs one on himself.

We're led over to a pair of jet skis and I climb onto one as the rental guy gives me instructions on what to do if we fall off or if it stalls out. Then we're turning them on and slowly cruising out onto the lake.

Jet skiing is my favorite. I lose track of time or my fears as Gavin and I fly across the water. He tries to splash me with his wake and I laugh as I chase after him.

After a while, I notice that I'm almost out of gas and we both reluctantly head back to the dock.

"Still think that you're cursed?" Gavin asks as we turn in the life vests and head back to his Jeep.

"Yep," I say simply, but I'm starting to have doubts.

Surely if bad luck was going to hit me, it would be when we were a hundred feet up in the air or racing across the water. Nothing happened though. Is that just a fluke?

We climb back into his Jeep and head farther down the road.

"Where are we going?" I ask when I notice that we're headed away from Destiny Falls and toward the center of Maple Bend.

"I thought that we would grab a bite to eat," he says easily and I relax.

Then I see the Ferris wheel and the other lights from the carnival, and my stomach drops.

"Just let me kill you," I tell him as he parks, and he laughs.

"Come on, chicken!"

I follow him up to the front entrance. He pays for our tickets and then drags me through the crowd to a stage.

"What's this?" I ask him as he hands someone some money and they pass him a clipboard.

"It's a hot dog eating contest."

"What?" I ask as he grabs my hand and tugs me up onstage.

"You don't have to compete, but I thought that it could be fun."

"You want me to shove hot dogs down my throat? Think of the choking hazard!" I hiss at him, and some teenage boys next to me laugh and elbow each other.

I roll my eyes at them, and Gavin hands me a bib. I reluctantly tie mine on as he does the same.

An announcer grabs the mic and my face heats as he goes over the rules and the clock is set to a minute.

"It's just sixty seconds. What could go wrong?" Gavin asks, and I glare at him.

"On your marks, get set, go!" the announcer yells, and I grab a hot dog and take a bite.

Gavin grins at me as he grabs one and we have to be the only two in this competition who aren't trying to win.

I laugh as he grabs a second one, and I reach for one too. We make it through one and a half each and are officially declared the losers.

I laugh as Gavin grabs my hand and drags me off the stage and farther into the carnival. I can tell that he wants to ask me if I still believe that I'm cursed, but instead he leads me over to the Ferris wheel and helps me on.

I expect him to ask at some point on the ride, but instead, he turns to me and kisses me. I close my eyes, getting lost in him and the sounds and scents of the carnival.

The ride stops and Gavin pulls back from me. We're both slightly out of breath, our lips red and swollen. I take his hand this time and we wander around, checking out some of the arts and crafts booths before we ride some more rides.

Gavin buys us popcorn, cotton candy, and an elephant ear, and we sit at one of the picnic tables and watch the kids and families walk by.

"Are you ready for the last activity?" he asks and I turn to him.

"Bring it on," I tell him, and he grins at me.

SEVEN

Record

"I CAN'T BELIEVE that you tipped me over," Gavin says with a laugh as we duck under one of the bay doors of his mechanic shop.

"It was only fair. I got wet, so you should have been too," I tell him and he grins at me.

"You got wet because a wave tipped your kayak over, not because I tipped you over," he reminds me and I try to hide my smile.

"Semantics."

He laughs and passes me my tote bag.

"Want me to throw your towel in the wash with mine?"

"No, that's okay. I can do laundry when I get back to Madelyn's place. I'll just hang it up somewhere to dry for now."

"Here," he says, taking the towel and heading into the lobby.

I watch him as he starts to hang up our wet stuff and

smile. Today was the most fun that I've had in a really long time. Maybe ever.

My phone buzzes in the tote bag that Gavin bought me at some little store near the beach. I have to fish around inside and when I finally grab it and see the screen, I'm starting to wish that I had brought it kayaking with us and it had fallen overboard.

There are over thirty missed calls from my family. I'm surprised to see that over half of them are from my younger sister. She never calls me unless she needs something, and I wonder if something bad happened.

Oh god, what if someone died or was in an accident? They could be in the hospital and I'm over here gallivanting all over town and drooling over some hot guy.

I'm just about to call her back when I notice the text messages.

There are over a hundred of them, and my heart races as I start to read. I'm expecting them to be letting me know that someone was hurt or passed away and asking me to come home, but that's not what I get.

Instead, it's message after message of them accusing me of ruining their lives and demanding that I return home.

They need my money to afford the mortgage and they were using my car to get around town. Now they're down to two, and my sister has been bugging my parents for rides to work or to borrow the car to go out with her friends and my parents stand it. They want me to buy her a new car. It's the least that I can do for messing up their lives and cursing everyone.

My stomach hollows at the familiar words and I start to feel numb.

They've been telling me some version of that sentiment for my entire life, and I guess I never questioned them. I mean, they're my parents after all and I just always trusted them and what they said. I'm sure that there's some psychological reasoning behind why victims blame themselves, and I wonder if I could ask Gavin's dad to explain it to me, but at the end of the day, I still believed it for over twenty-three years.

I think that Gavin was right.

I'm not cursed. There's no such thing as curses.

We make our own luck, and my parents and sister have always taken the easy road. They don't need to work hard or try for things. Not when they can fail, blame it on me, and then demand that I do something to make it up to them.

"I'm not a curse," I whisper to myself, my eyes stinging with tears.

"I know. That's what I've been trying to tell you," Gavin says softly from behind me and I hurry to dry my eyes before I turn to face him.

"My family has been texting and calling me," I tell him, passing him my phone.

I watch as he reads a few messages in the group chat, his features darkening and his fingers tightening with each new message that he reads.

"They're wrong. You don't owe them shit," he promises me, a fire burning bright in his eyes.

"I know. I'm starting to see that after today."

"Good."

He pulls me against his chest, and I go willingly, wrapping my arms around his waist as I breathe in his now-familiar scent of oil and pine trees.

"I mean, if anyone was the curse here, it was them. They held you back, tried to keep you tied down to their level," he points out.

It's amazing how just a few days away from them and I

can suddenly see things so much more clearly. Or maybe it's just that Gavin took the time to show me how wrong I was.

He's right. I don't need them. I'm so much better off without any of them in my life.

"Are you okay?" he asks as he pulls back slightly.

"Yeah, I am," I promise him, and he gives me a lopsided grin.

"Good. The last part for your car came in. Want to help me fix it? Then I can take you home or we can grab a late dinner or something."

"Sure."

I follow him over to my car and he grabs me a camping chair and sets it up nearby before he gets to work.

"It's cool that you know how to do all of this," I say.

He smiles. "It's not super hard. Once you've done a few, you're pretty much a pro," he says and I shake my head.

"I'm clueless about building and fixing things. It's cool that you're so self-sufficient."

His face heats slightly and I wonder if he's blushing or if it's just hot under the hood of my car.

"Do you want to learn?" he offers after a beat, and I'm tempted to take him up on it, but I shake my head.

"Nah, I'm enjoying the view too much," I tell him with a wink, and he grins at me, shaking his head slightly.

He doesn't seem to believe me, so I get comfortable in my chair and start to tell him what seeing him all greasy and sweaty does to me.

"I'm serious. The first time I saw you when you came to get my car, I literally said 'holy shit,' when I saw you."

He peeks up at me and I stare back at him.

"Then every time I see you in those coveralls or all sweaty and covered in grease. Whew!" I say, fanning myself and his cheeks turn a brighter shade of pink.

He grabs the new belt, and I watch as he partly disappears under the hood of my car.

"Have you ever thought about making a calendar and selling them?" I ask him, and he bursts out laughing. "I'm serious! I would even take the pictures for you."

"How generous of you," he says dryly, and I grin at him as he tightens the last bolt on my car and straightens up from under the hood.

"I'm a giver," I tell him, and he crooks a finger at me.

"Me too. Come here and let me show you."

I stand on shaky legs and make my way over to him. My heart is starting to beat faster as I approach him and take in a quick breath as I look up to meet his clear blue eyes.

Lust tightens like a fist around my throat and even though I have no experience here, I know that I need him.

I keep eye contact with him as I reach up, slipping the straps of my sundress down. The material sticks to my damp bathing suit and I wiggle slightly to free it.

"Fuck," he whispers harshly, and I smile as I see his eyes heat.

The dress pools at my feet and I kick it to the side. My flip-flops go with it and then I reach for the tie of my bathing suit on the back of my neck.

"Record," he says, and my heart kicks against my ribcage. "Are you sure?"

"Yes," I say instantly and it's like a flip has been switched in him.

He takes over, untying the straps at my hips until I'm standing before him naked. He reaches behind his neck and pulls his shirt off, tossing it over by my dress and then he's reaching for me.

He backs me up against the nearest vehicle, some newer model car, and I gasp as he pushes me back onto the hood.

"Gavin," I start, but he just shoots me a sexy grin and steps between my legs.

"I've got you," he says against my lips, and I nod.

He kisses me quick and then starts to trail kisses and nips down my neck. I wiggle and arch against the hood of the car, and he smirks against my skin as he licks a path up to my nipple.

As soon as his lips wrap around the stiff peak, I become possessed. My brain shuts off and I'm nothing but feeling.

He sucks and licks and nips at my body until I'm screaming his name, my hands trying to find purchase on the smooth hood of the car. Gavin kisses lower, his hands wrapping around my hips to keep me in place as he drops to his knees and buries his face between my thighs.

"Oh, shit!" I shout, and even though I can't see him, I know that he's smiling.

"That's it," he praises me, and I wiggle, trying to grind down against his face.

The dull throb that was pulsing between my legs has suddenly turned into an inferno. It feels like I'm being burned alive and I love it.

I come against his mouth, screaming his name, and then he stands, leaving me boneless on the hood of the car as he pushes his swim trunks down and pushes my thighs wider.

"Are you sure?" he asks, his mouth still wet from my juices and his eyes a little crazed.

"Oh yeah," I breathe out. He grins at me as he grips my thighs.

I bite my bottom lip as I feel the tip of his cock brush against my folds and I wonder if I should tell him that I'm a virgin but before I can decide, he thrusts into me, burying himself deep inside of my clenching channel.

His eyes widen and he stares down at me.

"Record... shit, I'm sorry. I had no idea," he says, and it looks like he's in pain.

The sting that came from him popping my cherry is gone now, and I wiggle, trying to take him deeper.

"Fuck," he curses, his hands tightening around my thighs as he stops me from moving.

"It feels good," I tell him, my voice coming out more like a moan.

"It's your first time. It shouldn't be on top of a car," he tells me, but I shake my head.

"I think it's hot. Do you not want to fuck me?" I ask, and he looks torn.

"Of course, I do."

"Then move," I urge him, and he closes his eyes.

It looks like he's at war with himself and I wonder which side will win. Finally, his eyes open and I know that I'm getting laid tonight.

"Fine. I'll fuck you on the car, but then we're going upstairs to my bedroom so we can do this right."

"Okay," I happily agree. He grits his teeth as he starts to move.

He pushes some of my blue hair out of my face and I arch, trying to take him deeper.

"Fucking perfect," he grits out and I reach up, grabbing hold of his biceps and hanging on as he starts to pound into me.

His hair is dark with sweat, or maybe just water from the lake still, and I look up into his blue eyes as he starts to rut into me.

He feels so good. I feel so full, and for once, I'm not worried about the curse or my parents or sister. I'm just living in this moment with Gavin.

I never want it to end.

I can feel a tightening in my belly though, and I know that it won't be long before I'm coming again.

"I'm close," I tell him, and he nods, his eyes locked on my face as he shifts, putting my legs over his shoulder and driving into me.

The new angle has him hitting my clit with each stroke and I swear my eyes roll back in my head as I burst apart.

"Gavin!" I shout and I hear him make a choked sound in his throat before he finds his own release.

He's still thrusting though and it has my orgasm going on and on. I sag back against the hood of the car, my body boneless. My eyes won't open, so I keep them closed as Gavin slowly pulls out of me and moves to the side.

I peek my eyes open and watch as he grabs his shirt off of the ground for me. I sit up and he drops it over my head, helping me pull my arms through.

"Now," I start, my voice coming out only slightly slurred. "Let's see this bed."

EIGHT

Record

"ARE you going to stick around then? You're more than welcome to stay with us!" Madelyn says as we head down the street.

"Yeah, I think so," I say, biting back a grin as Flynn backs up out of the driveway.

We're headed to Prim + Proper for a tasting. Hudson, Lyla's boyfriend and the owner of Prim + Proper is opening a new place in the next town over, Lilac Harbor, and he's settled on a menu that he wants everyone to try out.

I was a bit surprised that I was invited since I've only been in town for a little over a week, but Lyla insisted. It seems that I'm one of the gang already.

I can't deny that I love that.

I have friends for the first time in what feels like forever.

I never really opened up to Madelyn or Flynn in college. I was always too busy working or studying to really put too much effort into friendships. Or that's what I told myself anyway.

The truth is that I was embarrassed. I was a curse, something bad. Even my own parents couldn't stand me. How did I expect anyone else to?

Now I see how wrong that was. I've opened up a lot to my new friends here, and it's safe to say that they all hate my family. We got drunk one night, minus Iris since she's pregnant, and talked about our families. It was interesting to hear about Lyla and her mom and stepfamily. She doesn't talk to them now after the way that they treated her and I can't say that I blame her.

She's been encouraging me to go no-contact with my family too, and I have to agree with her. These past ten days have been the best in my life. I feel more relaxed and happier than I can ever remember.

I'm sure that a big part of that is Gavin. We spend every spare second that we can with each other.

He got the other part for my car, and I helped him install it. Then I told him that he looked hot all covered in grease and he proceeded to fuck me in the back seat of my car. It was a bit of a tight fit, but neither one of us was complaining.

He's meeting us at Prim + Proper and I can't wait to see him again. We grabbed lunch yesterday, so it's been almost twenty-four hours. This is the longest that we've gone since I first got to town, and I don't like it.

He's like a drug to me now. I need my sexy mechanic fix.

"Are you going to try to paint here? Or we could take a day trip to Sault Ste. Marie for the craft show one weekend or something," Madelyn offers and I nod.

"I'm not sure what I'll do yet. Iris was telling me about

some craft and market type sales down in Mackinaw too, so maybe I'll check those out too."

"You should do classes," Flynn says, and I turn to see him grinning at his own idea.

"Art classes?" I ask.

He nods. "Yeah, there's not much like that up here. I bet parents would pay you to do like a weekly class or something, especially during the summer."

"Yeah, he's right. You could make a killing," Madelyn says.

I blink. I've never thought about teaching. I was worried about getting close to kids and cursing them, but now that Flynn mentions it, maybe it is a good idea.

"I'll think about it," I say as we pull up outside of Prim + Proper.

Gavin is already outside, talking to Sutton and Teller, and I wave as I climb out of the back seat.

"Hey. Missed you," he says.

I grin. "Missed you too."

He brushes a kiss against my lips, and I smile.

"You're in a good mood," Gavin comments, and I nod.

"Flynn just gave me an idea."

"Yeah? What's that?"

"He said that I should teach art classes here in town."

I can see him processing that. Weighing the pros and cons and then he nods. "Yeah, that's a great idea."

"You don't seem happy," I say and he kisses my cheek.

"I am. I was just about to offer you a job with me."

"Doing what?" I ask with a snort. I'm terrible at cars, and it would take me years before I could be much of a help with him.

"Painting the cars. I've been toying with the idea of

expanding that side of the business, but it was just me, and I didn't think that I had time."

"Painting cars?" I say, blinking as I think about it.

I've never thought about that before.

"I suppose it could be fun," I say as we join our friends by the front door.

"What could be fun?" Lyla asks as she and Hudson open the front doors of the restaurant.

"Painting cars."

"Ohh, I'm in!" Lyla says and I laugh.

Lyla is up for pretty much anything. She said that she wants to try it all, and I love that she's such a free spirit.

"For Gavin's shop?" Sutton asks, and I nod.

"Yeah, you should do it. I think that you would be great at it," Iris says with a smile.

"We'll see," I say, turning to grin at Gavin, but my eyes snag on the figures over his shoulder and my stomach and smile both drop.

"Mom?" I ask, not quite believing what I'm seeing.

"What?" Gavin asks, turning with a frown to see what I'm staring at.

"That's my mom... and my dad and sister," I finish as they all climb out of the old SUV that I remember all too well.

They look so much older, and I wonder how that happened. It's only been a few days, but they seem to have aged years.

My mom is still pretty with her blonde hair and sharp blue eyes. She's where Callie and I get most of our features from. Callie got our dad's dark hair though, and her eyes are a darker shade of blue, like his. We both have her full mouth and small nose. I scrunch my own nose as they step out onto the sidewalk.

"Oh, really?" Gavin asks, his voice lethal, and I grab his arm before he can storm over there and tell them off.

Madelyn and Flynn move to stand next to Gavin, and everyone else lines up on my other side so that it's very obviously us versus them.

"Uh, hi," I say as they get closer to us.

"There you are," my mom snaps and I wince, my fingers tightening around Gavin's forearm.

That's a tone that I've heard too much from her, and I know what it means.

She's pissed.

"We've been calling and texting for weeks!" she snaps again, and I want to roll my eyes.

"I've only been gone for less than two weeks, so that's weird," I sass back.

That seems to take them all by surprise, and they freeze on the sidewalk.

I've never talked back to any of them. I know that it wouldn't have done me much good. Besides, it was the three of them against me. I was never going to win. Better to just take it and then escape when I could.

"What did you say?" my dad asks, and I straighten my shoulders as I look at him.

"What do you want? Why are you here?" I ask him instead.

He glares at me. "We came to get you. You can't just abandon your family. Not after all that we've done for you."

"You haven't done anything for me," I say, letting go of Gavin's arm and taking a small step forward.

"We raised you! We let you live with us after graduation!" he spits out, and I feel my fingernails bite into my palms as they tighten into fists.

"No, I moved back because you needed me to work to afford the mortgage!"

He takes a step toward me, and Gavin grabs my hand. I know that he'll pull me back if my dad or anyone in my family gets much closer to me, and having him on my side only has me feeling more confident.

"I never liked the house, and it's not mine, so I'm not paying to live there. I've moved out and I'm not coming back. Not ever," I state firmly.

No one says anything for a beat, but I can see my parents sizing me up and trying to find a weak spot.

"I know that you were stealing from me. That's why I had a different hiding place and a secret bank account. I've been putting half of my paycheck there for years so that you couldn't touch it."

My mom frowns at that, her eyes flashing. I know that they've been taking from my "secret" hiding spot in my room, but really I set that up so that they would stop asking me for money.

My sister, Callie, steps forward. She looks pale and maybe even a little sad. I'm surprised because she always just seemed to go along with my parents, and whatever they said or did to me, she did too.

"Can I talk to you for a minute?" she asks and Gavin's hold on me tightens.

"Um..." I start and he looks over to me. He shrugs and I nod. "Okay."

We walk a few steps down and she turns away from our family, giving them her back.

"Please come back," she whispers and I blink at her.

She sounds like she's crying. I don't know what to do in this instance. I've never seen Callie cry.

"I can't take it any longer," she says and tears start to

really come then, spilling onto her cheeks and rushing down to her chin.

"Can't take what?" I ask.

What could our parents have been doing while I was gone?

"I can't take being you!" she sobs.

I blink. "What?"

"Ever since you've been gone, they've been treating me like they did you," she admits and she looks up at me with red, miserable eyes.

"Oh... yeah, I guess you can't be the golden child when they need a scapegoat," I say, and she starts to cry harder. "I'm not coming back, Callie. Never."

She looks down to her shoes, trying to wipe the tears away.

"So, you knew that they were treating me like shit then?" I say when I realize what she said.

She nods. "Yeah, I'm so sorry. It was just easier to go along. They seemed to love me more when I started doing it," she admits and I take a step away from her.

She notices and looks up at me with real regret swimming in her eyes.

"I'm so sorry, Record I've been a terrible sister. I should have helped. I should have told them to stop or something. I just... couldn't."

I'm probably never going to be able to understand why she didn't help me, but I can't leave her with them. Not when she's sobbing like this after only being alone with them for a few days.

"You're eighteen. You can move here with me until you start college in the fall," I offer.

"Mom and Dad will never pay for my college if I don't stay with them."

"I hate to break it to you, but they don't have money for their own mortgage. There's no way that they're paying for college."

She sniffles and I let out a deep breath.

"You can still go though. Do what I did. Take out loans then. Work and save your money. Maybe see if you can get financial aid or some scholarships. Hell, pick a cheaper school."

She nods, looking away from me.

"It's that, or get back in that car with them and drive all the way back to Grand Rapids."

She actually turns pale at the thought, and I wonder just how bad things have been at home since I left.

She takes a deep breath and then nods as her eyes meet mine.

"Do you know anywhere that's hiring?"

"I might," I say with a small smile and she gives me a tentative one in return.

"We'll have to find an apartment or something. I've been staying with Madelyn and Flynn."

She nods and then surprises me by stepping forward and wrapping her arms around me.

"I'm so sorry. I know that it doesn't make up for any of it, but I promise that I'll always keep trying to make it right."

I squeeze her back and nod against her head.

"Let's get rid of them."

She nods and lets me go, and we head back to where my friends are still facing off against my parents.

"Callie is staying, but you can leave," I tell them and I watch as their eyes widen and their nostrils flare.

They were not expecting that and they're not happy with the news.

"Absolutely not. Both of you, get in the car. Now!" my

father snaps, and I shake my head, my hand squeezing around Callie's.

Gavin takes my free hand and squeezes, urging me on.

"We're done with you."

With that, I turn, taking Callie and Gavin with me. Hudson opens the restaurant doors and we all file inside, leaving my parents standing on the sidewalk, fuming.

As soon as the door is locked behind us, I turn to Gavin and wrap my arms around his neck.

"I'm so proud of you," he says as I cling to him.

"Me too," Madelyn says, and I smile as she wraps her arms around Gavin and me.

I laugh when Flynn, Sutton, Teller, Iris, Arlo, Lyla, and Hudson all join in. We pull back and I see Callie standing there, looking unsure.

I'm still not sure about all of this either, but I don't regret inviting her to stay. Maybe we can finally fix our relationship and even be friends now that our parents aren't here to mess it up.

I look over Gavin's shoulder and smile as they slam the car doors and squeal off down the road.

"Guys, I want to introduce you to someone. This is my sister, Callie. Callie, this is my new family."

Everyone grins at that, and I take Gavin's hand again as we head over to the table that's been set up.

"Hey," Gavin says, stopping me before I can sit down.

Everyone else is still introducing themselves to my sister and so we have a moment of privacy.

"I'm alright," I tell him before he can ask and he smiles.

"I know you are. You're so strong. Your parents never stood a chance," he says and I warm at his words.

"Thanks. I couldn't have done it without you."

"Yes, you could have."

I feel tears sting the backs of my eyes and I squeeze his hand.

"I love you, Record," he says and I suck in a sharp breath, staring at him with wide eyes.

"What?" I choke out.

"I love you. I know that we haven't been dating long, but I know how I feel about you."

"How?" I blurt out and he grins.

"You were cursed with such a big heart. I couldn't help but fall in love with you, Rec."

I can't hold the tears back then, he reaches up, helping me brush them away.

"I love you too," I admit, and he grins.

"Yeah?"

"Yeah. How could I ever not love my sexy mechanic?"

He laughs at that, pulling me into his arms and I go gladly.

This right here, this is my home. I feel safe and loved when I'm in his arms and I know that he's right, we haven't known each other long, but I know how I feel with him. He's it for me.

It's crazy to think that if I hadn't have broken down here, I may have never met.

Thank God for curses.

NINE

Gavin

FIVE YEARS LATER…

"WHERE'S RECORD AND CALLIE?" Lyla asks as soon as she opens the door and I roll my eyes.

"They're coming right behind me," I assure her.

She nods, smiling down at where my daughter, Ivy, is fast asleep in her car seat.

"Did she just fall asleep?" she asks.

I nod. "Yeah, on the way over here."

She waves me inside and I follow her through the house and onto the back deck. It's the last day of summer and everyone decided to get together for a barbeque. We're over at Lyla and Hudson's place since he was doing most of the cooking, but I can't complain. They live right on the water and their house is huge, so there's more than enough room for all of us.

"Hey, man," Flynn says as I set Ivy's car seat down in the shade on the deck.

"Hey, how's it going?"

He's got a kid half asleep on his shoulder and I smile as she starts to drool on his shirt.

"Pretty good. You're the last to arrive. Where's your better half and Callie?" he asks, and I grin.

I married Record four years ago. I knew that she was the one for me after our day together breaking the curse, but Record had a lot of memories and other things to work through. The first summer she was here and living with Callie was pretty rough for her. She's been in therapy ever since her parents left town, and that's actually where she is right now.

Sometimes she and Callie do group therapy, both of them trying to work through the trauma of their childhood. They've both come a long way. Callie went to cosmetology school and works at the salon over in Lilac Harbor. She lives there with her husband. She actually just got married last year and had Record as her maid of honor.

Both sisters cut off their parents and have only grown closer over the last five years. I couldn't be prouder of her, of both of them actually. They've both come so far from when I first met them, but I know that it hasn't been easy for either of them, especially Record. So many things that her parents and sister told her, or rather blamed on her, had to be untangled.

She opened up to me when we were dating more, and every time she did, I would hold her while she cried and reassured her that she did nothing wrong. There were still times when she would try to pull away from me because she was convinced that she was going to hurt me, or rather the curse was. It was hard to see her beat herself up, and I vowed to kill her parents if they ever came near her again.

They haven't. I think that they got the message the last time that they were here because they haven't tried to reach out since. Last we heard of them, they had lost their house and had left Michigan and headed south. Neither girl tried to find out where they went. They were both just happy to be done with them.

I was worried that their lack of a bond or connection would hurt Record, but she's made a new family here, one who loves and supports her no matter what. Callie has become her biggest cheerleader and I know that it means a lot to Record.

There are still times when Record blames herself or stresses about the curse. The first time that I got hurt fixing a car when she was around was a big one, but we've worked on it a lot in the last five years, and now she seems to be better.

The trauma and lies that her family put her through took a while to untangle, but she's happy now and an amazing mother to our little girl.

Ivy stirs in her car seat and I move to unbuckle her as the front door opens and Record's familiar blue hair comes into view. Callie is right behind her, and I stand and give a small wave as they head my way.

"Hey," I greet my wife, and she grins at me.

"Hey, sorry I'm late."

"We just got here too," I tell her. She leans up to kiss me.

Ivy reaches for her right away and I let Record take her from my arms.

"How's my little baby?" she coos at Ivy and I smile as I watch them interact.

Record is exactly the type of mom that she deserved, that we all deserve. She's patient and loving. She would do anything for our girl and for me, and I know that I'm damn lucky to have her as my wife.

"Did you miss Auntie Callie?" Callie coos at Ivy and she laughs, smacking her hands together.

"That's a yes then, huh?" Record says with a laugh.

"Want me to take her?" Callie asks Record, and she kisses Ivy's head before she passes our baby to her sister.

We watch them head down the back porch steps to the beach to join our friends and I pull her into my side more as we follow slowly.

"Your mom called me on the way over here. They're thinking about putting an offer in for a house here in town."

I nod. My parents love Record, Callie too, and ever since we got married, they've been talking about moving closer to us. Once we had Ivy, they talked about it a more, so I'm not surprised that they're finally going to do it.

"That will be nice. They can watch Ivy for us and we can go out for a date night," I say, nuzzling her neck, and she beams at me.

"Uh, we can watch her too!" Lyla interrupts.

I kiss the top of Record's head before we turn to face her friends.

"Yeah! We should set up some weekly or biweekly babysitting routine so that we can all get a little break," Sutton says and I can already see her starting on the project in her head.

"Sounds like a plan," I say as I lead Record over to where Callie and Ivy are sitting at the patio table.

I pull out a chair for her, and she smiles as she takes a seat. Ivy is busy looking around the backyard, her eyes wide and locked on the water. We both think that she's going to be a swimmer because she's always absolutely fascinated by it.

We actually just put an offer in for a house a few doors down from Lyla and Hudson. We probably won't hear back for a few days, but I think that we have a real shot of getting it.

It will be nice to be close to our friends, and I know that both of my girls want to live by the water.

Record started her art classes the first summer that she was here and they were a huge hit. She loved working with the kids and creating new class plans or pieces of art. We ended up going up to Sault Ste. Marie for some of the craft festivals and she sold some of her pieces there as well.

Once the summer was over, I taught her how to paint cars and she loved it. She has a schedule now where she does three art classes a week, usually at night, during the school year, and helps me out at the shop an additional two days a week.

The mechanic shop has taken off since she joined. I'm more organized, and with her doing bodywork, I can focus on the engines. We ended up hiring someone a few months before Ivy was born, and I'm glad that we did. We could use all of the help that we can get now that our little one is here.

"Who's ready to eat?" Hudson calls, and Lyla grins as she holds up a bowl of potato salad.

"I'll make you a plate," I tell Record as she takes Ivy back from Callie.

"Thanks."

"Anything for my best girls," I say, giving both of them a kiss before I stand to help my friends.

I was always the loner, the one who was happy to get his hands dirty. I never thought that I would have a wife or a kid. No one ever really interested me.

Not until I met Record.

From that first meeting, I was intrigued, and that only grew with each day that I spent with her.

Now I'm cursed with an amazing wife who is smart and strong and loving. One who gave me a beautiful daughter and who makes me laugh like no one else. One who is my partner in everything, who truly is my better half.

It's quite the curse, and I thank the universe every day that she cursed me.

WANT A FREE BOOK?

You can grab Sweets Here.
**Check out my website, www.shawhart.com for
more free books!**

ABOUT THE AUTHOR

CONNECT WITH ME!

If you enjoyed this story, please consider leaving a review on Amazon or any other reader site or blog that you like. Don't forget to recommend it to your other reader friends.

If you want to chat with me, please consider joining my VIP list or connecting with me on one of my Social Media platforms. I love talking with each of my readers. Links below!

Website
Newsletter

A Very Mountain Man Christmas

A Very Mountain Man New Year

Folklore

Kidnapping His Forever

Claiming His Forever

Finding His Forever

Rescuing His Forever

Chasing His Forever

Folklore: The Complete Series

Holiday Hearts

Be Mine

Falling in Love

Holly Jolly Holidays

Love Notes

Signing Off With Love

Care Package Love

Wrong Number, Right Love

Kings Gym

Fighting Fire With Fire

Fighting Tooth and Nail

Fighting Back From Hell

Mine To

Mine to Love

Mine to Protect

Mine to Cherish

Mine to Keep

Mine to: The Complete Series

Sequoia: Stud Farm

Branded

Bucked

Roped

Spurred

Sequoia: Fast Love Racing

Jump Start

Pit Stop

Home Stretch

Telltale Heart

Bought and Paid For

His Miracle

Pretty Girl

Telltale Hearts Boxset